from

puppy love
by
Eric Hill

PUFFIN

PUFFIN BOOKS
UK | USA | Canada | Ireland
Australia | India | New Zealand | South Africa

Puffin Books is part of the Penguin Random House group of companies
whose addresses can be found at global.penguinrandomhouse.com

Everyone
needs
puppy love...

Spot

all the
time,
everywhere...

but especially...

*when you
feel like...*

a kiss...

or a
cuddle...

whether
you're feeling
happy...

or sad...

when you're
on your own...

*waiting for
a call...*

or in a crowd...

having a
ball...

whether
you've been
naughty...

or as good
as gold...

whether
you're young
or whether
you're old...

puppy love
is what
you need!